GW00341065

I Wish...
Some More

Some more wish poems by John Dean

with illustrations by Erik Sansom

For Judith,
More best wishes,
John Dean

HB
HARVEY BOOKS

I Wish... Some More © 2007 John Dean.
johnmichaeldean@yahoo.co.uk

Published by Harvey Books.
First Edition 2007.

Illustration by Erik Sansom
esansom@sympatico.ca

All rights reserved. No part of this book may be reproduced, stored in a retrieval system or transmitted in any form by any means (electronic or mechanical, through reprographic, digital transmission, recording or otherwise) without the prior written permission of the publisher.

Typesetting and repro by Publishing Solutions.
www.publishingsolutions.co.uk

Printed in Spain by MCC Graphics on FSC paper.
www.mccgraphics.co.uk

ISBN 978 0 946988 82 X

For Grace

Contents

From Harvey Books

By the same author:

Stuff and Nonsense.
A book of verse for children,
first published in 2006.

I Wish...
Wish Poems,
first published in 2007

Acknowledgements

Assistance in editing was provided by Victoria Smith and Lucy Dean.

"I Wish I had a Jabberwock" is based on the poem
"Jabberwocky" by Lewis Carroll.

The idea behind "I Wish I could be Dutch" was provided by Tom Dean.

William Roe suggested the design for the back cover.

Kevin Inskip's many years in the Merchant Navy provided inspiration
when composing "I Wish I was an Ocean."

Claire Hummerstone, a maths student, provided inspiration
for "I Wish you could be Couth."

"I Wish I had a Drop or two of Eddie's Ring-Bo-Ree" is based on
the fifth verse of "The Jumblies" by Edward Lear.

Introduction

I wish you well
In all you do,
My best wishes are
In here for you.

Welcome to my second book in the "I Wish" series. If you read the first you will know that there is at least one star to be found in each illustration.

Some of these illustrations and poems will make you think. Try matching the books with the ologies in "I Wish I could Master an Ology" and the part illustrations in "I Wish I was an Illustrator" with the full illustrations throughout the book. Eddie is Edward Lear in "I Wish I could have a drop or two of Eddie's Ring-Bo-Ree"and the boy in the illustration has everything mentioned in the fifth verse of Lear's poem, "The Jumblies," apart from the Ring-Bo-Ree. The writing on the carton in "I Wish We owned a Chinese Take-Away" does say something. It is nothing deep and meaningful, but you might need to investigate. And in case you have never heard of it, a muu-muu is an Hawaiian form of dress.

Of course, some of these wishes are more realistic than others. "I Wish I Lived on Io" is a wish of my own, but I never expect to fulfil it. I leave it for you to decide if "I Wish I could Write Poems" would also be appropriate in my case.

I would love to hear what you think of the book. Please e-mail me, but remember to use the e-mail address of your parents or guardian. Further copies can be ordered from my e-mail address, as can copies of the first book in the series, "I Wish..." and copies of my earlier book of verse for children, "Stuff and Nonsense."

My continued good wishes,

John Dean.
johnmichaeldean@yahoo.co.uk

I Wish...

...I was a Wizard

I wish I was a wizard,
I would always get my way,
I'd wake up in the morning
And have a perfect day.

I'd magic all my teachers
To sit upon the roof
And get my know-all brother
To never know the truth.

I'd turn my nasty neighbour
Into a slimy toad
And place his house upside-down
A mile along the road.

And if people start to argue
Or are apt to say, "Tut! Tut!" —
I'd cast another wizard's spell
And zip their mouths right up.

...We had a Hippopotamus

I wish we had a hippopotamus,
I'd keep it in the bath –
It would be so much fun for us,
We'd really have a laugh.

I think I'd call it Buster –
A thing so fat and wide –
And I'd use a feather duster
To brush its underside.

...We owned a Chinese Take-Away

I wish we owned a Chinese Take-Away —
I love my sweet and sour —
I'd stay at home through night and day
And constantly devour.

But it wouldn't be the same —
The customers would find
That we would quickly change its name
To "The Chinese Leave-Behind."

...I could master an Ology

I wish I could master an ology,
Be it psycho or geo or zoo —
I might even try biology —
Any ology on Earth, it will do —

Palaeontology, campanology —
Escapology would be fun —
Astrology, ecology, neurology —
I'd be happy to learn any one —

Methodology, theology, archaeology —
All these ologies in contention —
Myology could be my ology
If it's within my comprehension.

It doesn't matter, I make no apology,
I have in mind no specific area —
An understanding of any old ology
Would make the whole world seem less scarier.

...I could do a Full Lotus

I wish I could do a full lotus,
Touching forefingers with thumbs at the tips,
But I know I don't stand the remotest
Chance with my dodgy hips.

The art of yoga, when you apply it,
Should take you to realms of elation,
But all I get whenever I try it
Is an extremely painful sensation.

...I could eat Ice Cream

I wish I could eat ice cream,
But it sets off some reaction —
Of its taste now I can only dream,
I must endure dissatisfaction.

The doctor says if I take one lick
It could be the last thing that I do —
Come on, pass me that cornet, quick —
I think it's worth the risk —

Oh, poo!

...I had a Stream

I wish I had a stream
That flowed across our lawn –
This has been my dream
Since the day that I was born.

I'd spend hours there just fishing –
Such a relaxing thing to do –
There is no harm in wishing,
But I wish it would come true.

Affected by the gentle flow
I'd rest in total peace –
I'd watch the ripples come and go,
I'd gain complete release.

I'd dangle both my feet
In the water to keep cool –
It would be my special treat
When I get home from school.

...I could smell like my Dog

I wish I could smell like my dog —
Not his smell, but a similar sense —
My dog smells more like a hog,
But his olfactory skills are immense.

From a distance I could smell my dad
And all the odours in between —
Hold on! I must be mad! —
This would surely be obscene.

...I had a Jabberwock

I wish I had a Jabberwock,
I'd keep it in a cage —
Under key and under lock,
To contain its savage rage.

Catching and biting the food that I give it,
Whiffling and burbling all day —
Nevertheless I'd have a good time with it
And I might even teach it to pray.

It would stare at me with eyes of flame
When I'm doing comprehension —
I'd treat it well, and yet to maim
Would be its sole intention.

...My Dad was not so Hairy

I wish my dad was not so hairy,
He's an embarrassment on the beach –
Some people find him scary –
We should keep him out of reach –

On a little island of his own,
Leave him there and count our losses –
Then the only things left to moan
Would be crabs and albatrosses.

...I was a Humming Bird

I wish I was a humming bird
Suspended in the hall —
I'd be fine, you can accept my word —
And I'd never fret at all.

My dad would take me for a walk
Or should I say a hover,
And if he'd rather stay at home and talk
Then he wouldn't have to bother —

I could fly around and wait
To go out with my mum —
As long as it was not too late
She could take me for a hum.

I'd lick things from the jar,
I'd sleep above the bed —
They'd be proud, would be Ma and Pa —
I'd be fine, it must be said.

...I was my Teddy Bear

I wish I was my teddy bear;
I'd get cuddles night and day;
My feelings I would learn to share
In a very loving way.

I'd get kisses from my owner;
I wouldn't have to steal one;
I'd no longer be a loner
For my friend would be a real one.

...I could be Dutch

I wish I could be Dutch –
They are the tallest nation.
Why do they grow so much? –
Well here's my explanation –

Their homeland is very low,
But at seventy-two inches and a quarter
The average Dutchman has learned to grow
Above the flooding water.

...I had a Muu-Muu

I wish I had a muu-muu
Instead of top and jeans –
I need a sudden breakthrough
To improve my dress routines.

Walking in a muu-muu
I would not be missed
And if I avoid all doggy do-do
I might even end up kissed.

...I Lived on Io

I wish I lived on Io,
Its volcanoes spewing phosphorus,
I'd be shouting, "Me-o my-o!" –
My future would be prosperous.

Above me in the sky –
The giant planet Jupiter.
O wow! O me! O my! –
It would be super-dupiter!

...I had Fur or Feathers

I wish I had fur or feathers,
I could dispose of clothes,
I could go out naked in all weathers
Covered up from head to toes.

Spots and wrinkles would not show,
I'd look the same when I grow old,
And it would be excellent to know
That I'd never feel the cold.

Make-up and facial creams –
I'd confine them to the past –
The advantages, or so it seems,
Would be many and they'd last.

And if I wish it for everyone
It would be the end of fashion –
A soft and cosy life of fun –
Oh, I want it with a passion!

...I had Digestion

I wish I had digestion
So I could stomach what's discarded –
Please consider my suggestion –
It deserves to be regarded.

Mould and maggots – they're a sin! –
Please grant my wish with haste –
But I'd also need another bin
Where I could dump "my" waste.

...I was an Adult

I wish I was an adult –
I'd keep me back from school,
And to give me something else to do
I'd buy a swimming pool.

I wish I was an adult –
I wouldn't tell me, "No!" –
And if I came in mucky
I'd simply say, " 'Ello!"

I wish I was an adult –
I'd let me stay up late –
I wouldn't make me clean my room
And give me things I hate.

I wish I was an adult –
I'd care for me a lot –
I wouldn't say, "Now, sit up straight!" –
And answer me with, "What?"

I wish I was an adult –
I'd let me sniff and scratch –
I'd never say, "Don't burp!" – "Don't whine!" –
"Don't whinge!" – "Don't run!" – "Don't snatch!"

Yes, if I was an adult
These things I'd try on me,
Not bothered by those who say,
"What an awful man is he!"

...I had a See-Saw

I wish I had a see-saw,
I could keep it in the garage –
My parents should have allowed for this
When they contemplated marriage.

"Children must come first in life!" –
That's what good people say,
And since my parents aren't bad people
They should let me have my way.

...I was an Ocean

I wish I was an ocean
Or else a massive sea –
This is a funny notion,
But it's what I want to be –

Tranquil and turbulent,
From grey to azure blue –
Unpredictable, resurgent
And soaking wet right through –

Unfathomable and rolling,
A mystery with purpose –
A barrier, thus controlling
Some of those who would usurp us –

Powerful and furious,
Stormy and at rest –
Such a mixture and so curious,
Of all things to be – the best.

Wide and deep and surging,
Forever wild and free –
I am therefore urging
You to grant this wish for me.

...I had a Set of Lights

I wish I had a set of lights –
All drivers then would pay –
I'd make it well within my rights
To stay on red all day.

In fact, what I'd really like
Are red lights front and rear –
Then I could go on my bike
At all times without fear.

...I was Venusian

I wish I was Venusian
And not a thing of Earth,
Having taken Venusian elocution
Lessons since my birth –

And if I was Venusian
I'd take time, I wouldn't hurry –
Coping with pollution
Without the need to worry.

Living in that seething heat,
But immune to pain,
Dangling my Venusian feet
In pools of acid rain.

...I was a Flamingo

I wish I was a flamingo,
All elegant and graceful –
Down my throat the food would go,
Faceful after faceful.

I'd really like to try it;
It would be fun, I think –
And I could always change my diet
If I get sick of being pink.

...I had a Dragon

I wish I had a dragon
To call my very own,
I'd put a great big tag on
It so my parents wouldn't moan.

I do tend to lose things, see,
And a dragon would have value –
I'd take it out for walks with me
And if you're lucky it would smell you –

If you're not then you could end up toast,
But such is life! – *C'est la vie!*
And I have to weigh up what I want the most –
Fun for you or fun for me.

...I was an Angel

I wish I was an angel,
I'd let my wings unfold,
I'd fly up to the highest height,
A wonder to behold.

And if I was an angel
I'd only know of good,
I'd only ever do the things
That little angels should.

I'd be a special angel,
I'd help the human race,
Presiding over matters
With a kind angelic face.

...There was a Shop for every Item

I wish there was a shop for every item
And arranged alphabetically
From Land's end to John o'Groats –
How delightful that would be! –

Wigs from Inverness,
Feather beds from Thruxton,
Cabbages from Exeter,
Jelly beans from Buxton –

Motherwell for sausages,
Liverpool for llamas,
Accrington for pepper pots
And Nelson for pyjamas.

But we'd have to curb our shopping,
Plan it mile by mile,
For if we had a lot to get
We could be gone awhile.

...You could be Couth

I wish you could be couth,
For a person you're disgusting –
A revolting smelly youth
Whose habits need adjusting.

You pick your nose, you sniff –
But I wouldn't swap you for another –
Despite the awful whiff
You are my little brother.

...I could save the Avocet

I wish I could save the avocet –
It is struggling to breed –
On the water's edge it cannot get
What waders really need.

With rising tides year by year
It has nowhere left to wallow –
It may be the first to disappear,
But eventually we'll follow.

...I could be Lemon Curd

I wish I could be lemon curd,
I'd enjoy myself so much –
I know it would be quite absurd,
But my love of it is such –

That my appreciation of every other spread
Has rapidly diminished –
So let me lick myself instead
Until every drop is finished.

...I Lived beside the Nile

I wish I lived beside the Nile
When the pharaohs reigned supreme,
To visit there for awhile –
That would be my dream.

I saw it on the TV screen
And all its glories beckoned –
Perhaps I could be a queen
To Rameses the Second.

...I was a Hyena

I wish I was a hyena
Laughing all day long.
Life for me has been a
Bore – and that is wrong.

But I'm sure, as a hyena,
With my speckled spots and stubble,
That I could perform a misdemeanour
Without getting into trouble.

A fully-fledged hyena
Is what I want to be –
In my dreams I've never seen a
More fun-filled role for me.

...I had a drop or two of Eddie's Ring-Bo-Ree

I wish I had a drop or two
Of Eddie's Ring-Bo-Ree;
It's what I need to see me through –
It would do the trick for me.

Life is very dull in Staines
Now sadly I've conceded –
And so, to alleviate the pains,
Something else is needed.

...I was Australian

I wish I was Australian,
But I wouldn't be a person –
Marsupial, not mammalian –
The antipodean version –

A kangaroo, a koala bear,
A wallaby would do –
How marvellous to be living there,
And you could live there too.

...We had a Volcano

I wish we had a volcano
Sat in our back garden,
To see the lava flow
And very slowly harden –

It makes good soil, they say,
So we'd still get lots of flowers –
From my window I would watch the spray
Through many endless hours.

...We could keep Koi

I wish we could keep koi –
Of these carp I am so fond –
And I won't be a happy boy
Until we've got some in our pond.

I like the way their bodies glide,
Their beauty is extensive –
I'd care for them with pride,
But Dad says they're too expensive.

Each one is like a fishy gem,
All bright and ornamental –
So if we can't afford them
We should take some out on rental.

...I could cut the Mustard

I wish I could cut the mustard,
I mutter and I murmur –
I'm a hopeless fat Great Bustard
And I can't leave *terra firma*.

To take off I'd need the rate
Of an Olympic sprinter,
But I haven't, and I can't lose weight –
So I'm stuck here for the winter.

...I had a Giant Slide

I wish I had a giant slide
From my bedroom to the grass –
One that's several metres wide
And made of shining brass.

Dozens of times a day
I'd go down and race back up –
My friends and I would play
Until it's time to sup.

I'd be very popular again
After problems with the pool –
Life can be so brilliant when
You're given something cool.

...I was a Surgeon

I wish I was a surgeon –
Not medical, but tree –
A new talent then emerging
And that talent would be me.

I'd trim trees into different shapes:
A camel, an aeroplane,
A shoe, a bunch of grapes,
A 3-D view of Spain –

Cooked eggs (both boiled and fried),
A star, a hot-cross bun –
Journeys through the countryside
Would be terrific fun.

...I was a Sacred Cow

I wish I was a sacred cow,
My subjects there to treat me –
And they would simply not allow
Anyone to hurt or eat me.

I'd be well-fed, and healthy
In muscle, skin and bone –
Well-adorned and wealthy,
Sat high upon my throne.

...I was an Architect

I wish I was an architect,
I'd re-design our city,
And when you come to inspect
You'd find it very pretty –

With bits that twist and twirl
Projecting overhead –
I'm such a clever girl –
It would be great, it must be said –

With windows in the shape of stars
And a park upon each roof,
With routes through buildings for the cars –
You'd cry out wow and 'struth.

And way up on the highest hill
I'd build a white acropolis –
With my efforts our city will
Become a great metropolis.

...I was an Illustrator

I wish I was an illustrator,
I'd paint pictures everywhere –
On the table, on the radiator,
On the baby when he's bare –

On the wall of the conservatory,
On my father's cotton vest –
I'd get everyone to worship me
And say that I'm the best.

...I could write Poems

I wish I could write poems,
But rhyming and metre and scanning seem totally
beyond me.
I keep trying to produce a good one,
But, despite all my efforts, I never seem to be able to get
anywhere.

I am hoping one day it will come to me,
That I will get the knack –
But on the other hand, the way things are going at the
moment
I might just change my mind and give up altogether.

Wish List